Joy

René David

Paperback ISBN 979-8-9919360-3-3

"Cash or credit?" I whispered, wanting to scream: *Speak up guys!*

Dead silence.

"The Usual Suspects," as everybody called the servers, interrupted the silence. Barney placed a French onion soup with sizzling croutons and melted cheese atop Tara's paper place mat. *Is she taking pics and texting?* Katz handed a juicy brisket sandwich to Monchi. *Is he filming, as well?* Carmen and Ms. Russ placed a matzo ball soup and a dry pastrami platter in front of Obi, before massaging his broad shoulders. *The lucky bastard, gets all the attention!* Tomasa and Monchi guzzled mimosas through big pink straws. *¡Ridículos!* Apparently, they'd arrived way before the rest of us got here at six. And finally—my fries! Ben shoved my loaded French fries onto my greasy, wrinkled mat. *They're burned! ¡Coñó, increíble!*

"Your sis is just fine, Sunny," Ben had the nerve to whisper in my ear. *My sis is fine, my ass. She hasn't said a word in months.*

"Why do I keep coming to the 8th Ave Deli if I don't get no respect here? Unbelievable!" I said laughing out loud.

"Handsome, they gave you my soup by mistake! Can you pass it to me s'il vous plait?" Fina Morgabin begged of Obi, caressing his shoulder. *Is she texting that picture she just took?*

"What the bleep happened to you all that you don't talk anymore but instead send me emojis, GIFs and weird videos?" I was beginning to see a pattern between all these people and Joy.

I accidentally knocked over a water glass, staging a Swan Lake scene with ice cubes spread all over. And everyone lowered their heads, interlacing their fingers on the table. All except Fina Morgabin, who stared at me defiantly.

"Is Joy dying?" I asked.

2

Dead silence once again.

"This is nonsense! What's wrong with Joy?" I shouted, staring at my miserable, charred fries.

"What's wrong with *him*?" Fina whispered to Obi GigaPunch, a hacker and MMA fighter, who was also turning into a pretty good masseur. *I think Fina likes him.*

They all raised their cells, showing pics and clips Joy had sent.

"I haven't seen her much lately and she hasn't been as chatty, though…" said Obi, attacking a chunk of pastrami.

"So she talks to you!" I asked.

"Sure, but not much," answered Obi, winking at Fina.

"She messages me all the time with emojis but I'm a bit tired of that nonsense," I said, raising my hand to get a server's attention. "Why doesn't she *talk* to me?"

"Her use of emojis is very clever. Have you noticed that?" asked

Monchi, smiling at Tomasa. *What's going on between these two?*

"But I am not an emoji interpreter nor do I communicate well with

symbols. I'm an actor. I speak lines for a living."

"He suffers from adaptability syndrome," Fina murmured to Obi,

who chuckled. *I heard that, ma'am!*

"Just emojis!" interrupted Tomasa, sipping her drink while leering at

Obi. Can a yogi become a sommelier? *Who are you trying to fool,*

borrachita?

"Pics, lots and lots of cute pics I see. Nothing wrong with it, mates!"

Fina flashed her gorgeous eyes at me.

"All I see is vids, clips, and emojis!" I barked, my frustration rising.

Fina's geranium eau de parfum made me feel nauseated, but just

then, Carmen, the server, saved me by placing a plate of crispy, cheese-wrapped pickles on my stained place mat.

"He's so irritable, isn't he?" Fina whispered to Obi. *Again?*

"Haven't seen you in a while…. getting bigger by the day," Carmen said.

"I've been auditioning out West, that's why," I replied.

"You put on some weight, Sunny. That polo shirt doesn't fit you. Or, well, your girl is fattening you up, isn't she?" *And there she goes, singing "Weird Al" Yankovic's "Fat."*

"Obesity could be due to a negative core belief," Fina muttered, glancing at everybody but me. *Who is she talking about?*

Tara cut in, chewing on a slimy onion. "Joy is a busy woman, and her son is a handful."

"He's only twenty-two. Perfectly normal. He still has plenty of time to grow up. On the other hand . . ." Fina began, looking at me.

What?

"So, the shrink just declared a war on maturity," I muttered, scooping the croutons and melted Gruyere off of Tara's soup. She was so nice, she didn't even blink.

"Well, her son is in a serious relationship with a woman. Did you know that?" Tara power-cleaned her cheeks and blouse with her pink napkins.

"If I don't hear it straight from the horse's mouth, you'll have to fill me in. I need your help," I insisted.

"Okay. She doesn't want to talk. She moves instead," said "handsome" Obi, as he extended his hairy, muscular arm and foraged through my burnt fries.

"Even at our Cinco de Mayo lunch, she only ever answered by shoving her phone in my face," Monchi said.

"Isn't that what most people today do?" Fina asked.

"Indeed!" Tomasa replied. "But didn't she ask about bubblies for a wedding?"

"No, she just waved colorful vids for every question we asked," said Monchi.

"Who's tying the knot?" I asked.

"At least she's moving again and even choreographing a version of *Les Noces*," said Tara.

"The Wedding? That's creepy," I said. "At least no one real is getting hitched."

"The ballet, yes, and that's beautiful," said Fina.

"Drunk, I can watch anything," said Tomasa.

"I'm with you on that," I agreed.

"Bloody hell! Cut Joy a break!" Fina yelled, startling me. She brought her cup of soup to her plumped up lips. *I think she works as a shrink for the elderly . . . although, didn't she quit recently because she's caring for someone who's transitioning?*

Katz handed a plate of frankfurters to Tara, placed a beer on my damp mat, and a glass of bubbly on Tomasa's. And of course, everyone went back to texting again.

"You seem to love your rosé, don't ya?" Dr. Morgabin asked.

Tomasa nodded with a smirk.

"This is me—give me a ring!" Fina handed her business card to Tomasa. *Why? Not enough clients? Desperate for company?*

"I mean, it's true that Joy has become an expressionless human being," Tara went on, biting her weenie.

"She is fine. She's in all sort of therapies, champs!" said Obi.

"Botox, maybe?" I suggested. "Did she have something done at the dentist?"

"No, no, no, my cuz is just fine. Look!!!" said Dr. Morgabin, pointing at her tablet.

Did I hear Fina calling my sister her *cuz*? Is she now claiming to be our *hashtag* relative? I liked her, but what was with that affected English and strange, ducky French accent? She opened her tablet and flipped through screens and screens of Instagram and Twitter, displaying unusual hashtags:

#DoIt! ... #EmojiQueenJoy ... #OnionSoupFrickPic ... #AnimatedJoy ... #PastramiAverXion ... #Wed@Reunion ... #ShutTheFlip&Selfie ... #DateTonightFilmMe ... #BrisketLoser ... #ShutUp&Pic! ... #ShutUp&Pin! ... #ShutUp&Tag! ... #ReuNionParty ... #PitIsHere!

"Joy's animations? Any clue, you guys?" I asked, noticing that all the hashtags had the same handle: @JoyMomShutUp&Love, my sis.

"Yes, but don't you guys worry. I'll ask a cyberpsychologist friend about her behavior," said Fina.

"She needs a shrink?" I asked. A second of silence was broken by a group of noisy folks marching through the doors. "Repeat Fina!"

"They're actors from my troupe. We come here after rehearsals for beer and weenies." Obi laughed.

"You're acting, too?" I asked.

"My girl invited me to her group. Even Joy approved, champ." He waved at the troupe.

"Your girl?" *I didn't think of that, but it makes sense a guy like him wouldn't be alone.*

"Here they come!" growled Monchi.

"And the babka with ice cream?" asked Carmen.

"Me, me, me!" Tara raised her muscular arms, snapping pics left and right. "Hashtag Yum … Yummy!"

"That babka has alcohol in it?" asked Tomasa.

"Nope! Just brioche dough, cacao and leche, hashtag DELICIOSO!" Tara said around the spoon in her big mouth.

"We must intervene, folks…. My sis … your cuz?" I pointed at "exotic" Fina. "Your bestie is losing it! Damn it!" I screeched. "Where're my fries, coño?"

"I already intervened. I hacked her phone, and she's just in a back-and-forth with a guy," said Monchi.

"A guy?" I asked.

Carmen, though, interrupted me, placing an egg cream atop Monchi's spotless place mat. *Is he going sober now, really?*

"How'd you get into her account?" I asked, a bit insulted.

Carmen suddenly went flying into the air, legs up, her bum slamming onto the floor. She'd slipped on a puddle of water next to me. I jumped to help while Monchi yapped but Carmen only gave me a hateful look and disappeared, never to return to our table. *Bummer! I really like her.*

"As I was saying, I hacked her damn phone while she was in the bathroom," Monchi went on and on with that demonic laughter. No wonder why he hasn't worked in months. Bum! He has this weird arrangement with his ex where she lets him stay in her home to care for their spoiled twins Madoc and Mat.

"Monch! Enough, man!" I yelled but he kept slurping on that disgusting, slushy soda.

"Look, we're stuck here!" yelled Obi pointed at the window.

Outside, the streets had darkened, and a torrent of rain poured down without compassion.

Fina stood up, left a few singles at the table and marched to the door.

"Cheap," I muttered.

"Cheerio, kiddos. Au revoir, à la prochaine!" she called.

"What the fuck is she saying?" I muttered, watching her leave. Drenched in rainwater, she looked like a pollo mojado.

"Kiddos, I need a drink!" I shouted.

So, I ordered one too many pitchers of beer and shots of bourbon for Tomasa, and we all toasted many, many times to Joy and to us and to Fina not falling into a pothole crossing the street and drank until the last drop of rain fell around midnight. I finally asked Ben to take the cold, burned fries he'd never replaced off the bill.

"Thanks for footing the bill, Obi. You're the man," I said. "Thanks, Tara, for leaving a *huge* tip. Well, after all, I'm the one who comes here all the time. No wonder Joy is attached to you guys. You're awesome!"

Heading back to my studio in Jamaica, I couldn't sit still on the J train. I laughed and cried the entire subway ride. I was confused but ready to intervene on Joy's behalf. I was eager to see a change in my sis or a change in my perception of life. I went to bed with more questions than answers about Joy, her friends, and even myself.

* * *

Our intervention occurred weeks later, when Joy's friends agreed to meet me at Tip your Sombrero, a hidden Mexican restaurant in Hell's Kitchen. Dr. Morgabin and Tomasa insisted on renting a private lounge in the basement and paid for hors d'oeuvres and margaritas. It was a nice move, but I would have been happier going to my 8th Ave Deli instead. I really wanted to chat with Carmen—someone with both feet on the ground—and maybe ask her out.

"What's up with Fina?" I asked.

"Joy didn't tell you?" asked Obi.

"Joy?" I asked surprised. "She sent me a whole bunch of emojis, but I gave up trying to decipher them."

"Fina is rehabbing after a biker struck her on 8th Avenue," said Tara.

"She survived?" I asked.

"Yes! A biker banged her from behind. She didn't see it coming," said Tomasa.

"But of course, it was pouring that night," I said.

"She's fine! She's with her fiancé! Dr. What's-His-Name?" said Tomasa raising a glass of pink seltzer water.

"Just water?" I shouted, cry-laughing like one of Joy's emojis.

"Yes, they're tying the knot soon in her native Réunion, so you'll probably get an invitation to fly there." said Obi.

"Marry?" *I'm not made for the New York pace.*

I was eager to see Joy and exchange a few words with her. I was also hopeful that she would be eager to speak with me in front of her best friends.

Joy arrived, dressed in a dark palette: socks, dress and shawl. Even her typically dyed blonde hair was black—unheard of for her.

My sis brought an iPad, a Kindle, AirPods on, and—*wait a minute*—

a pager? Nooo! Two different phones that she placed on top of a

solar bag. She was also wearing glasses. *Whoa! Google spectacles?*

She'd brought the arsenal, come prepared for war.

We all sat right across from her—four of her besties and me, her bro.

Fina, the shrink, was missing in action. For some reason, I kept

thinking she would show up at any moment.

They'd all come from Tomasa's yoga class. Monchi wore green

Lululemon tights and a pink jacket. Tara revealed her chunkiness

through thick leggings and a see-through blouse, and she wore a cute

French beret. You had to see it to believe it! She and Monchi were

wrapped around each other like a pretzel, kissing and all. Obi still

wore his white massage therapist uniform, and Tomasa, who was

glued to him, wore that Margot Robbie Barbie pink dress. A rose was

tucked behind her left ear. Nice! I'd dressed light—a bit boring, but

not even Joan Rivers would remember who I was wearing.

Everybody had noticed the sudden change in Joy's wardrobe. I'd been told that she'd been dressing head to toe in dark colors for a month, and her makeup was also gradually shifting toward a somber look—dark eye shadow, black lipstick, tattooed brows.

Just like Tara, Joy had been an exceptional dancer, touring with lots of troupes, until she fell from a horse on a New Paltz farm, and, la pobre, spent three long months bedridden. When we visited, she looked like a battered woman: always sad, her black-and-blue arms, face, and legs covered by bandages. She couldn't utter a word, had trouble hearing us, and couldn't recognize any of us for a while.

Once she got out of bed, she obsessed over her son, my nephew, Tonos. She fretted about his strange online friends, particularly his girlfriend, Tomy La Purée, a cute Korean violinist and foodie Instagram sensation, who wanted to raise a ton of kids on my parents' farm.

All of a sudden, my sis stopped talking. But she started sending me messages with her new persona, Avatar Joy. She sent me videos of black horses, ponies and alpacas. She seemed obsessed with equestrian affairs and cartoon farm animals. Lately she'd been clogging my WhatsApp account with clips and GIFs. I would call her, but she never picked up, even when I knew she was at home. She'd been out of work for a while, but she'd recently gotten a part-time job recording books for the visually impaired. If she was only communicating through her gadgets, I wondered how she managed there.

Then "Avatar Joy" started leaving me emojis of a horn, a piano and a book, and I gathered that meant she was on her way to record audiobooks. More and more emojis of hand gestures came into my WhatsApp, emojis with tongues out, a brain and a ninja, which I thought meant that she was on a mission to save the world with this new gig.

I got so worried that I called my parents and asked them to intervene. I loved my adoptive parents to death, but they were too quirky and silly, and their extremely dark sense of humor knew no limits. So, they were my last resort. My parents were shrinks, though. Great doctors! But they never applied any psychology to us. We'd always been free-range, raised on their farm near Cherry Grove Blind Valley. Well, I arrived from Florida when I was thirteen-ish. In their "Finca Pollo"—as they christened it, because my hair would frizz up like a chicken—I would play with their pollos, goats, and my parents' beloved ducks, even though they were smelly and noisy as hell. But like everything else, I quickly grew tired of them: Disgusting monsters!

Anyway, our servers, Gil and Hagos, filled up our glasses with water. As Joy opened her mouth and pulled a tablet from her tote, two gorgeous ladies hurriedly started placing a sizzling feast on the large table.

"Fuck!" Joy shouted. *Whoa!* That put a smile on my face.

She blushed and shut her mouth.

The aromas were fabulous. Fajitas, brisket empanadas and Mexican gefilte fish—which was Tomasa's idea. She was Oaxacan and had insisted on ordering it for us. There was matzo ball pozole soup for Tara, and, of course, tortillas and chunky guacamole for everybody else. And ah! Frozen margaritas with *Salicornia* and limes.

"Salud!" I toasted and they all followed—even Joy.

Well, my sister sipped her drink and smiled a bit. She played videos of Tonos singing "Ave María" and Tomy La Purée accompanying on the violin. It was adorable. We all clapped. But she didn't even say thank you.

Tara was about to say something, but Joy pressed her tablet screen and our phones all clicked, as did the laptop inside my mochila.

We all heard strident and extremely loud chanting, and right after that, a Stygian black horse rode from my screen to Tomasa's. It blurred on Monchi's screen, but reappeared on Tara's, only to finally fall off a blind cliff on Obi's phone.

Tara threw her arms around Monchi's neck and started bawling. I couldn't help but join in. *What was my sis trying to say? Was she suicidal? Was she mourning the loss of a friend? Someone we didn't know?* She'd been very friendly when she was still dancing. I'd often thought she had way too many friends. *Or was it all about her ability to communicate?* She saw people when she read for the visually challenged, so then what was she not telling me?

Our servers came back.

"Hola, is everything going kosher?" asked Gila while Hagos uncorked a bubbly.

"Yes, yes, Hagos, please pour in!" Tomasa raised her glass, winking and even throwing him a kiss. *Back to wine, missy?*

From behind the black curtains, two tall figures emerged.

My parents: Mr. and Mrs. Kazal appeared, sporting the brightest smiles. I hadn't seen them since Thanksgiving, when I visited their poultry farm—to which they had added more than a hundred rescued alpacas.

"Surprise, kiddos!" they yelled, which wasn't typical of them. "Is the funeral over!?"

Behind my parents stood a short man sporting a black coat and dark glasses. *Google spectacles? Yeah!* He opened the curtains with the help of a bamboo cane.

Joy stood and said: "This is my Piton but his real name is Lucas Morel. He's my fiancé."

My sis was talking at last, but too loudly and making large, sweeping gestures. She was tapping on the floor and stomping big-time. I thought she was dancing again.

"Piton and I met at the recording studio, and we've been friends since. Then we went out for tea, and we kissed and fell in love. And we've been playing games on his laptop. . . ."

"Bravaaa!" I mumbled.

We all smiled and teared up a bit.

"Piton is a Moringue fighter, a Sega drummer, a computer whiz, and an animator. He has animated my life. He has shown me how to love again through technology. But now I'll silence myself."

Piton grabbed her waist, and as they walked off, Joy turned and said, "I'm leaving my spot in the recording studio. You may find what you're looking for there."

Joy winked at me and disappeared behind the black curtains.

Acknowledgements

To Esperanza, my mom ... each night she came up
with bedtime stories.

To Yvette, my wife, my inspiration.

ABOUT THE AUTHOR:

RENÉ DAVID

Education:

New York University School of Continuing and Professional Studies, Certificate in Medical Interpreting.

Instituto Politécnico José Antonio Echevarría, La Habana, Cuba. Bachelor of Science, Maritime Transport Engineering.

Membership:

Cuban Association of Artist Artisans (ACAA) Asociación Cubana de Artesanos Artistas.

Professional artist:

Owner, Rene David Gallery: group shows, single artist shows.

Genres: Photographer, Painter, Sculptor, Interior Designer, specializing in country and rustic interiors. Natural Fiber Sculptures, including traditional folk basketry and contemporary original architectural woven sculptures.

Creator, writer, choreographer, dancer, vocalist, and performer of original interdisciplinary performances pieces and plays for educational presentations.

Professional occupation:

Spanish conference interpreter and instructor.